Licensed exclusively to Top That Publishing Ltd
Tide Mill Way, Woodbridge, Suffolk, IP12 1AP, UK
www.topthatpublishing.com
Text copyright © 2015 Tide Mill Media
Illustrations copyright © 2015 Emma Levey
All rights reserved
0 2 4 6 8 9 7 5 3 1
Manufactured in China

Written by Sally Hopgood
Illustrated by Emma Levey

ISBN 978-1-78445-288-9

A catalogue record for this book is available from the British Library

See You Later, Alligator

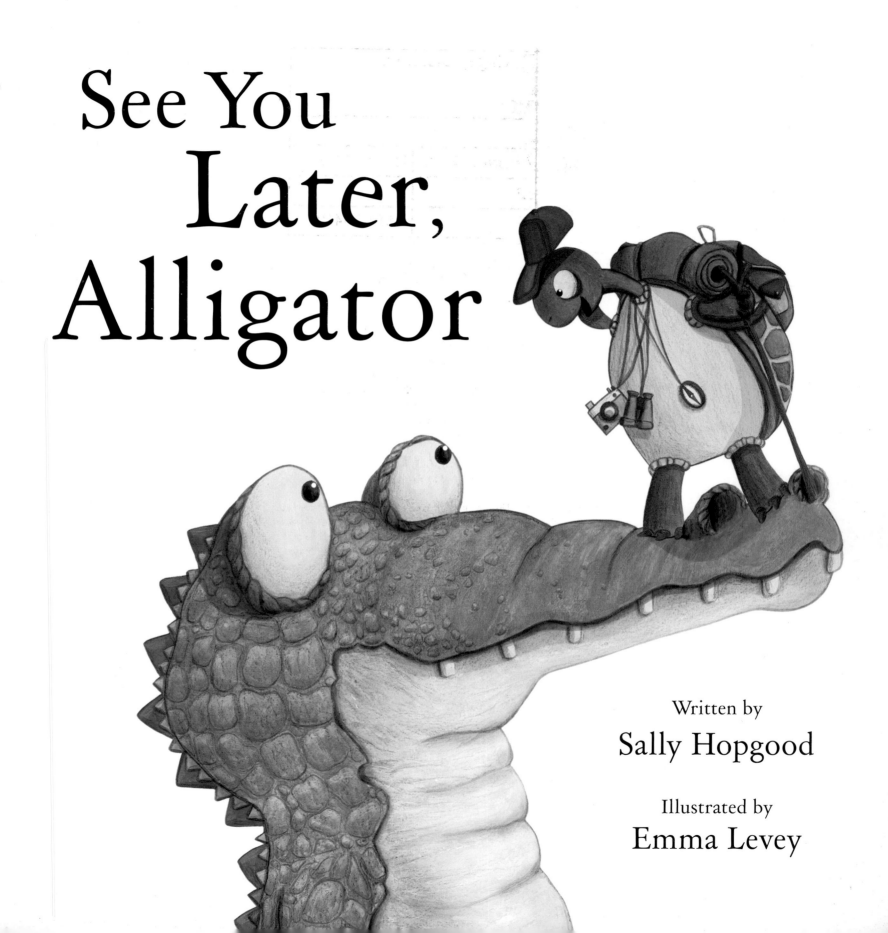

Written by
Sally Hopgood

Illustrated by
Emma Levey

Tortoise wanted to go on a big adventure to see the world. But he couldn't possibly leave without saying goodbye to all of his animal friends ...

See you later, **Alligator.**

Toodle-oo, Kangaroo.

I'll call you soon, Mr Raccoon.

I'll be gone before noon, **Mrs Baboon**, because ...

It's a long way there,
Baby Bear.

You'll have to stay here,
Little Deer.

It's over that hill, **Buffalo Bill**.

Through marshy bog,
Scruffy Dog.

And desert dry,
Butterfly.

Look after the house,
Timid Mouse.

The key's under the mat, Pussy Cat.

I've put money in the meter,
Anty Eater.

I'll be back, Natterjack.

Sooner than you think,
Slinky Mink.

There's so much more to see and do, **Mr Gnu.**

So don't wait up, **Buttercup**.

Looks like it's time to go, Slowly Joe.

It was the same every day. By the time Tortoise had said all of his goodbyes, the park gates were locked and his big adventure to see the world would start all over again the very next morning ...

'Is he still here?'